*"Everyone wants to be famous,
everyone thinks they're great
and most aren't."*
—Simon Cowell

American Idol™

The Official Book

The Search for a Superstar

Marissa Walsh

BANTAM BOOKS

NEW YORK • TORONTO • LONDON • SYDNEY • AUCKLAND

AMERICAN IDOL: The Search for a Superstar

The Official Book

A Bantam Book/August 2002

TM FremantleMedia Operations B.V. and 19 Television Ltd.
Based on the TV program *American Idol—The Search for a Superstar* produced by FremantleMedia North America
Licensed by Fremantle Brand Licensing www.fremantlemedia.com/licensing
www.idolonfox.com

Special thanks to Liney Li, Barbara Perris, Matt Walker, and Samantha Wolfe!

ISBN: 0-553-37599-7

Visit us on the Web! www.randomhouse.com/teens

Published simultaneously in the United States and Canada
Bantam Books is an imprint of Random House Children's Books,
a division of Random House, Inc. BANTAM BOOKS and the
rooster colophon are registered trademarks of Random House, Inc.
Bantam Books, 1540 Broadway, New York, New York 10036.

Book design by Liney Li   PRINTED IN THE UNITED STATES OF AMERICA   OPM   10 9 8 7 6 5 4 3 2 1

"This show is about this dream. That's what this show is about. It's about a young person's dream. A young person who has the stamina, the talent, and the passion to be judged by America—as well as the judges—week after week. And in the end, possibly for the rest of their lives. It's not easy but the payoff is worth it. This show makes a young person's dream come true. *American Idol* makes someone a star." **—Ryan Seacrest, co-host**

Everyone wants to be a star. Everyone dances around their room in front of the mirror when no one is around, singing into their pretend Pez dispenser/pen/hairbrush/water bottle microphone. And most people sing in the shower, too. Though the songs might be different, the desire is the same—everyone wants their 15 minutes (or seconds) of fame. But so few people who want to sing, act, dance, or make people laugh (on purpose) actually make it. Which is why we love *American Idol*. These guys are actually *doing* it. And their microphones are real.

Welcome to American Idol: The Official Book!

From the U.K., the country that gave us the Spice Girls and *The Weakest Link,* comes *American Idol.* What better place than the land of opportunity for such an amazing one! The U.K. version of *American Idol, Pop Idol,* was a national phenomenon, with 13.1 million people (over 50% of the viewing audience) tuning in for the last episode. The *Pop Idol* winner, Will Young *(right),* and the runner-up, Gareth Gates, have been shattering U.K. sales records right and left with their debut singles. We're betting the winner of *American Idol* does the same thing here.

A QUICK RECAP, FOR THOSE OF YOU WHO HAVE BEEN WATCHING SUMMER RERUNS

We've been watching with bated breath since June 11, waiting for Simon—the mean judge you've all heard about—to say something like "I think you just killed my favorite song of all time." Simon "Mr. Nasty" Cowell, and the other judges, Paula "Straight Up" Abdul and Randy "No, I'm not related" Jackson, saw 10,000 Britney and Justin wannabes in 7 cities and chose the best 121 to go to Hollywood for the next round. (Actually, they were only looking for 100 but they found so many talented people that they sent an extra 21 to Hollywood!) In Hollywood the judges had the daunting task of narrowing the field to 65, then 45, and finally to the 30 who would compete on the TV show *American Idol.* Each Tuesday night a group of 10 contestants sang for the judges and the viewers at home. And since it's *our* idol, after all, we, the people, got to phone in and vote. (Yes, we know, Ryan and Brian—during the two hours immediately *following* the show.) Don't worry; we got busy signals, too. The top three vote-getters were revealed the following night, on a *live* show, and moved on to the final round.

Our 10 finalists then shared a bathroom *and* a stage as they all lived together in a house and performed live every week in front of a studio audience and our favorite panel of judges.

Eventually, we will be left with two finalists, one of whom we will choose as the American Idol. Is this a great country or what?

Ryan Seacrest
Age: 27
Hometown: Atlanta, Georgia

What's up with those two guys?

Why, they're our spiky-coiffed tag-team $hosts$, Ryan Seacrest and Brian Dunkleman. Ryan provides the narration, asks the probing questions, and wears the great shirts. Brian is funny and always quick on his feet with an off-the-cuff remark. Their job is to give the viewers at home a break from the tension of the performances and the judges' critiques, but they also serve as a buffer and a sounding board for the contestants. After the contestants sing and go up against the terrifying trio, they can retreat to the comfort of the incessant clapping, hugging, and hand shaking that is the Red Room. Ryan and Brian dry the tears and build up bruised egos. And they really do seem to care.

Ryan Seacrest is no stranger to hosting duties. Host of the #1-rated weekday afternoon talk show, *Ryan Seacrest for the Ride Home*, on Los Angeles radio station Star 98.7 FM, Ryan has also had hosting stints on the following TV shows: *Ultimate Revenge*, *The Click*, *The New Edge*, *Wild Animal Games*, and *Gladiators 2000*. He once guest-hosted E's *Talk Soup* and even voiced the part of "Fighting Families Host" in an episode of *Hey Arnold!* back in 1996. E! Online was on the mark when they named him one of Hollywood's 20 Under 30 to watch. We're watching!

Brian Dunkleman is a stand-up comedian and actor who has appeared at the U.S. Comedy Arts Festival in Aspen, CO, and in Las Vegas. Incidentally, he once hit it big in Vegas at Caribbean stud poker for $13,000 and change. Brian has guest starred on *That '70s Show*, *Friends*, *The Hughleys*, *Third Rock from the Sun*, *Dharma and Greg*, and *Two Guys and a Girl*.

Brian Dunkleman
Age: 30
Hometown: Buffalo, New York

"Randy?" "Paula?" judges

One of the best parts of *American Idol* has been watching our panel of in action. *Simon*, whom the British press nicknamed "Mr. Nasty" during the run of the U.K. show, is clearly in charge. But Randy and Paula have their say, too. All in all, the group strikes a nice balance. They don't always agree, but they are always on the same side of the table. And at times they're no doubt thankful to have that table there.

As much as we all love to hate Simon, we all love to love Paula. She's kind and sweet, and after Simon's barbs, we appreciate her supportive presence. Together, she and Randy take away the sting.

Randy Jackson honed his constructive criticism and unflappable demeanor during his 20 years in the music industry. He was the vice president of A&R at Columbia Records for 8 years and senior vice president of A&R at MCA Records for 4 years. He has recorded, toured, and performed with *NSYNC, Madonna, Elton John, and Destiny's Child, just to name a few, so he knows a thing or two about American Idols. Randy has worked on over 1,000 gold and multi-platinum albums. His professional advice is invaluable.

WHAT HE'S LOOKING FOR IN AN AMERICAN IDOL:
"I think the main thing really for me is uniqueness, having a different unique style, a different sounding voice and also just having phenomenal talent."

Paula Abdul is herself an American Idol. She began taking dance lessons at age 7, won a scholarship to study tap and jazz at age 10, and got her first break in college as a Los Angeles Laker Girl. Since then, her albums have sold over 30 million records worldwide and her stats as a singer, dancer, and choreographer include two #1 albums, six #1 singles, a Grammy Award, seven MTV awards, two Emmy Awards, two People's Choice Awards, two Kids' Choice Awards, a star on the Hollywood Walk of Fame, and induction into the Nickelodeon Kids' Choice Hall of Fame. Whew! Her work as a choreographer includes Janet Jackson's videos, *The Academy Awards, The Tracey Ullman Show,* and the movies *Coming to America, Jerry Maguire, American Beauty, Black Knight,* and a new release, Dana Carvey's *Master of Disguise.* Paula also runs dance and cheerleading camps, competitions, and scholarship programs throughout the country. Having worked on and off-stage, Paula has a lot to offer as a judge.

Paula's Discography:
1988—Forever Your Girl
1990—Shut Up and Dance (The Dance Mixes)
1991—Spellbound
1995—Head Over Heels

Simon Cowell was one of the judges and stars of *Pop Idol,* the U.K. version of *American Idol.* Simon's career of shaping talent with tough love began in 1979 at EMI Music Publishing in the U.K. In the '80s, he formed his own label, Fanfare, along with a partner, and by 1989 BMG had offered Simon a position as A&R consultant. He recently set up his own label, S Records, through BMG.

The artists Simon has signed read like a *Who's Who* of pop success stories. Of course, you haven't heard of most of them because they're all English. OK, you may have heard of Five (who disbanded last year) and the global multi-platinum Westlife. In the last 10 years, Cowell has achieved sales of over 25 million albums, over 70 top-30 records, and 17 #1 singles. He's not all talk!

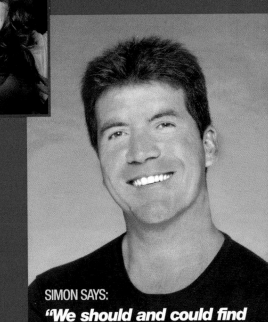

SIMON SAYS:
"We should and could find better talent in America."

Jaylen Moore

WHAT DOES IT TAKE TO BECOME AN AMERICAN IDOL?
A lot of talent and a lot of paperwork!
Here are just a few of the official rules
from the *American Idol* audition application:

Eligibility: You must be a **legal U.S. resident, 16 to 24 years old** on April 20, 2002, who is eligible to work in the United States. If you are less than 18 you must be accompanied to the audition by your parent or legal guardian. Please bring valid proof of age and a picture ID (for example, a birth certificate and a driver's license, a passport, etc.). You are ineligible if you already have either talent representation or a recording contract.

Material: Be prepared to **sing a cappella (without music)** a song of your choice. In the event you are called back for the first recall, you will be asked to sing two songs a cappella. One song must be selected from a list that will be provided to you by the producer prior to the first recall and the other song may be a song of your choice.

Paperwork: You will be required to **fill out, sign and agree** to all of the terms and conditions in our required forms. If you are found to have given any false information, you will be automatically disqualified.

NO WEAPONS OR NON-PRESCRIPTION CONTROLLED SUBSTANCES WILL BE PERMITTED AT ANY AUDITION.

Disqualifications: We reserve **the right to disqualify or exclude,** in our sole and absolute discretion, any individual from any of the auditions for any reason.

The Road to Hollywood

"A verse and a chorus, please."

The 10,000 *American Idol* hopefuls who auditioned in seven cities across America confirmed what we already knew: We are a diverse country full of undiscovered talent! How fun was it to watch Justin Guarini be discovered in New York for the first time? And Tamika in L.A. may not have been the best singer, but she could have a career in television ahead of her! And what about Elias and his T-shirt? Fashion designer, maybe? Of course, it was fun to watch the bad auditions, too, and that's where Simon comes in. We may have thought it, but he actually says it. He can be mean, but we enjoy Simon so much because his comments are clever, too. How does he come up with that stuff? Simon explains his role as a judge this way: "I'm here to do a job and I'm gonna do something which I think is going to be a shock to the American public. We are going to tell people who cannot sing and who have no talent that they have no talent. . . . You are about to enter the audition from hell." We can't wait.

LA

"Welcome to American Idol Smackdown."

In Los Angeles, the city of dreams, *American Idol* hopefuls camped out for a day and a half. But at least they don't have too far to travel if they are tapped for Hollywood!

THE GOOD: Ryan Starr is the first in L.A. to hear the magic words, "You're going to Hollywood!" after her rendition of "Lean on Me." Simon is not all insults. He has a way with the compliments, too: "I think you have a great talent."

THE BAD: Steven Ware earnestly sings "My Girl," to which Simon responds: "That was seriously terrible." Steven, confused, tries to sing some more but Randy stops him. "You may be, somewhat . . . there's a phrase called tone deaf."

L.A. is where we first meet Tamika. Yes, we all know by now: Ta-MEE-ka. After the judges break it to her that she will not be going to Hollywood (and they are actually somewhat gentle this time), she storms out with a few choice words: "Y'all got problems. Y'all got major

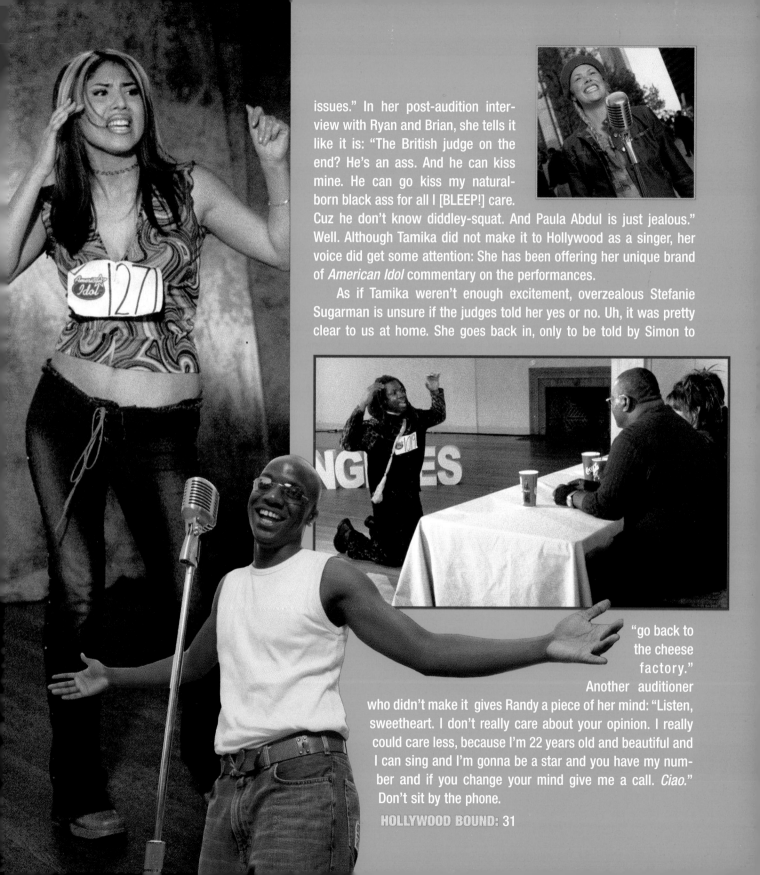

issues." In her post-audition interview with Ryan and Brian, she tells it like it is: "The British judge on the end? He's an ass. And he can kiss mine. He can go kiss my natural-born black ass for all I [BLEEP!] care. Cuz he don't know diddley-squat. And Paula Abdul is just jealous." Well. Although Tamika did not make it to Hollywood as a singer, her voice did get some attention: She has been offering her unique brand of *American Idol* commentary on the performances.

As if Tamika weren't enough excitement, overzealous Stefanie Sugarman is unsure if the judges told her yes or no. Uh, it was pretty clear to us at home. She goes back in, only to be told by Simon to "go back to the cheese factory."

Another auditioner who didn't make it gives Randy a piece of her mind: "Listen, sweetheart. I don't really care about your opinion. I really could care less, because I'm 22 years old and beautiful and I can sing and I'm gonna be a star and you have my number and if you change your mind give me a call. *Ciao.*" Don't sit by the phone.

Smells like teen idols.

It's still 1992 and grungy in Seattle, apparently, as we hear a Muzak version of one of Nirvana's greatest hits, with a few notes changed so as not to incur Courtney's wrath. The camera shows us that everyone is, like, pierced.

THE BEST: Karma Johnson is the first audition. She sings "Wind Beneath My Wings" and has a beautiful voice and presence. But Simon says that when he sees the words *American Idol,* there is an image and she doesn't fit it. Randy disagrees. She is going to Hollywood, where she will eventually be cut for the reasons Simon mentioned. Sigh.

A. J. Gil wants to be an American Idol because he wants to help out his mom financially. He sings the national anthem, inspiring a standing ovation from Randy! Our first and only. The Brit, too, says it is "fabulous." A.J. cries, in shock. He is a good guy. Another great audition comes from Trinity Manning. We're loving the kids in Seattle. She's holding a picture of her dad, who passed away when she was eight. She makes the cut.

THE WORST: Dude, the next words of "American Pie" are, "I can still remember." Remember them next time.

Levi Blue can't sing. "I just want to be somebody's product," he tells the judges. "I want you guys to re-create me." Simon picks up a pen. "Well, this is a pen, not a magic wand."

HOLLYWOOD BOUND: 10

"I don't think you'll ever be ready."

The windy city is abuzz for *American Idol* as a morning news helicopter shows half the Midwest lined up outside the audition, waiting for their turn to get turned down.

THE GOOD: Jacquette Williams has a great voice. Simon asks her if she thought she would go through to the next round and she says no. He asks why. "Because I'm a big girl." Well, she was wrong, she's going.

Jim Verraros is an "Up Close and Personal" waiting to happen. Both Jim's parents are deaf; he's fluent in sign language. But, since he's a singer, they have never heard him sing. He belts out (and signs) "When I Fall in Love," and earns a ticket to Hollywood.

THE I'M BAD, I'M BAD, YOU KNOW IT: Mark Scott is probably a nice guy but it is a little cheesy for him to say that "it would be selfish of [him] not to share his talent with [us]." We're busy people, Mark. His audition consists of imperson-

ating Michael Jackson, moonwalk and all. He is good, but is that enough? And isn't it so '87? The judges have their biggest fight to date over him. Paula loves him. She *did* do a lot of choreographing for the Jackson family. But she wins this battle and later calls Simon "unbelievably rude." Straight up. Come back and be yourself, Scott.

THE WACKY: The judges are getting restless. Paula is wearing a hat. A girl sings "Proud Mary" and Randy and Paula chair dance along. Ryan Farrar sings "Bohemian Rhapsody" and they all join in with Simon doing the "Mamma Mia" and "Galileo" parts. Ryan's infectious energy wins him a spot in Hollywood.

HOLLYWOOD BOUND: 23

"I can honestly say you are the worst singer in America."

THE BEST: Kelli Glover sings "I Will Always Love You" and Simon tells her that she has the "X factor with a capital X."

Justin Guarini is a force to be reckoned with. Not only does his performance make Paula swoon, it also inspires Simon to finally admit that American talent is better than English talent!

THE WORST: Rose can't handle the truth. Simon: "Your audition was horrendous." Paula: "I think your ambition outweighs your talent." Rose: "I wasn't trying to do the right notes." Randy: "You were trying to do the wrong notes?"

THE T-SHIRT: Elias! No one knows what to expect when Elias walks in in full "Zorro" getup, begins singing Britney's "Oops! I Did It Again!" and starts undressing. We are in Times Square, after all. The hat's gone, then the long black coat, revealing the best thing we've seen yet on this show—a T-shirt that reads "America will love Simon" with pictures of Simon on the front and Paula on the back. Can't see any of Randy. It's brilliant and hilarious and, more importantly, the three judges love it. Simon says that sometimes personality does count more than singing ability. Elias is stunned—and heading to Hollywood!

HOLLYWOOD BOUND: 25

ATLANTA

There must be something in the water in Atlanta because no fewer than three former beauty queens—Miss Atlanta, Miss Mississippi (runner-up), and Miss West Virginia/Canadian Oktoberfest—have shown up to audition. And one of them is 6'2".

THE GOOD: There is obviously some talent—and some devoted moms—in Atlanta. Jamar is the first audition and he nails it. His mom is there to celebrate. RJ Helton is next. He scores with a Jackson 5 song and runs out to tell his waiting mother. Third is John. He does well and wants to call his mother on Ryan's cell phone. But they can't get through. So someone else's mom pretends to be his. Are you feeling the love in Atlanta?

THE BAD: Paula and Simon have another fight over "patronizing." Paula says it with the long *a,* Simon with the short. Paula disagrees with the way Simon handles his criticism. The comment that put her over the edge was: "This guy can have 100,000 lessons, he cannot sing." The poor guy who inspired it is happy he wore his shades.

THE PRETTY: As for the beauty queens, Melanie Sanders moves on to the next round. Simon tells Tamyra Gray she is one of the best—"she goes beyond X to Zed." (*Zed* is British for the letter *Z*.) Unfortunately Miss West Virginia is not up to snuff. But she's pretty good for someone who began singing only last Monday.

HOLLYWOOD BOUND: 15

DALLAS

"Boring is wearing all black."

THE GOOD: Simon asks Dallas Cowboy cheerleader Kristin Holt what is more important to her: the Miss Texas pageant in July or *American Idol*. She gives the right answer. As she's running to the judges' table to thank them, she slips and falls flat on her back. Yes, she did sing "Fallin'."

Adriel Herrera goes for a different tactic. "Paula, you are so hot. For real," he tells her before singing his song. Simon gives him a choice: "It's Hollywood or a date with Paula." Adriel answers, "I have a better shot at L.A." We agree.

THE BAD: One hopeful won't take no for an answer. He sings and eagle-eyed Randy asks if they've seen him before. In L.A.? Yes. In Seattle? Yes. Either he has a lot of frequent-flyer miles or he's a glutton for punishment. Simon ensures they won't be seeing him in Miami: "You're still boring," he informs him.

The "Lady Marmalade" opera girl renders Randy speechless. But not Simon. "Have you taken singing lessons? Who's your vocal coach? Do you have a lawyer? Get a lawyer and sue her."

HOLLYWOOD BOUND: 11

MIAMI

"My name's Amnesia. Don't forget it."

Miami is the last stop on Randy, Paula, and Simon's talent-scouting tour. They are already over their goal of 100— will they add to it?

THE GOOD: Yes! Christina Christian knows who has the power. She sings "Isn't He Lovely" to Simon, which makes Paula puke. Then we have Alexandra and Tenia, the best friends. Alexandra sings "Genie in a Bottle." The judges clap. Tenia apologizes for sleeping under the air conditioner the night before. Excuses, excuses. But Simon is worn out; our country is big. Luckily for their friendship, they both make it. There is a lot of high-pitched squealing.

THE SAD: Anjela has been traveling on a Greyhound bus (a sad enough experience in and of itself), following the *American Idol* auditions across the country. She missed them in L.A. and Dallas and finally makes it to Miami. After all that, we want this poor girl to rock the house. She doesn't. She doesn't even have a song prepared; she says she is just going to sing whatever comes out of her mouth! The judges are kind. But she and her mom are getting back on that bus.

HOLLYWOOD BOUND: 6

HOLLYWOOD!

This is the big time. 10,000 auditioned; 121 were chosen. As always, Simon says it best: "One of you here is going to be the most famous person in America: the American Idol." If they can make it through the next three difficult days, that is.

"Chorus line from hell."

DAY 1: 121–65

Twelve groups of ten contestants each will now take the stage to face the judges. Each hopeful again sings a verse and a chorus and receives a critique, but must wait onstage until the other nine have sung before learning their fate. The judges aren't even using names in this round—just contestant numbers. Some numbers are asked to step forward, some aren't, and then your line is told it is either staying or going.

Jacquette from Chicago sings Aretha Franklin's "Respect" but doesn't get any from Simon. His problem with her is that she doesn't look like an American Idol. "Says who?" a bold Jacquette asks. Randy jumps in to ask Simon if Aretha looks like an American Idol. Actually, Simon doesn't think Aretha Franklin would win the competition if she entered now. Paula and Randy balk. Simon says he doesn't make the rules. We wish he could break them for Jacquette!

The judges have their 65. It's been a long day, but it's not over. The genders are split up to work with Lionel, the pianist. The girls will be singing "Say a Little Prayer" tomorrow, which will forever be associated with that Julia Roberts movie, while the boys will be singing "For Once in My Life," which will forever be associated with this show.

"Front line, you will be going home."

DAY 2: 65–45

The chorus line approach—and 56 people are gone on the second day of auditions. Today the kids have been broken up into groups of three, and each person in the trio has to sing the entire song while the other two do backup singing, dancing, and smiling. More importantly, Paula is again wearing a hat and her cute dad has come to visit! Today everyone is forgetting the words. It's not that hard, people. These songs are classics! Randy speaks for all of us: "I almost never want to hear that song again."

Joshua Crumpton from New York doesn't make it and is unhappy with Simon's comments. He says he did what he could with what he had to work with. Uh, from what we can tell, Josh had free airfare, a free hotel room, a

pianist teaching him the song, two other singers to practice with, and free advice from three music industry professionals to work with.

Khaleef Chiles from New York promises to work 10 times harder if he makes it. Promises, promises! The other three boys in his group have been busy practicing, but they lean toward the camera conspiratorially to give us the dish: Khaleef has never shown up to practice! All four move on, however, and one exclaims, "We have no idea what orifice we pulled that out of!"

Sixteen-year-old Natalie Burge from Chicago is confident beyond her years—she sings right to Simon and takes over the stage. Simon tells her that she came across as selfish but will therefore probably be a huge star. She moves on.

Max Lev, the self-proclaimed Broadway diva from New York, is sure that Randy hates him. He sang "If I Were a Rich Man" in his audition, so this could be true. His number is up. Also in Max's trio is Jules, who causes Simon to bang his head on the table and ask, "How can we judge you if you can't remember the words?" Since the judges criticized his look in L.A., Jules has been working on his image: He got his eyebrows waxed.

Trinity Manning from Seattle is in the last group, but this time she doesn't have her lucky charm picture of her dad. She doesn't make it through.

That's it for today. Eleven more are going home. But before they do, they have an audience with the judges. Who thought this was a good idea? Jules hogs the microphone and chastises Simon for breaking hearts, tells Paula he respects her, and invites Randy to work out at the gym with him. Randy reminds Jules that he's the one trying to be the superstar. Simon can't help himself: "You are here for one reason and one reason only—you are a loser."

"I have to compose myself."

DAY 3: 45–30

The 45 left had to learn another new song last night and will be taking the stage alone for the first time in this round of auditions as the rest of the kids sit in the theater to watch the performances.

Khaleef Chiles makes himself memorable by jumping off the stage to sing "Daydream Believer" to Kelli Glover from New York in the audience. Tenia Taylor makes herself memorable by wearing her self-described "hoochie shorts." Unfortunately, Akelee can't remember the words to "Save the Best for Last." It's a testament to what everyone has been through together that the kids in the audience help her out by singing along.

Now the judges deliberate. They start with the easiest: Justin Guarini, whose rendition of "Get Here" moved Paula to tears, and soon have their top 15. The next 15 are harder. Randy, Paula, and Simon look at headshots, argue, and drink soft drinks while the kids wait. Simon gets off some zingers: "I just think this guy is a waste of space." "He looks like a corpse and is so corny." Finally, the judges break the news to the happy 15 and then to the sad 15. There are hugs and tears in both rooms as this bonding, life-changing experience comes to an end. Friendships have been forged, critiques have been given, dreams have been fulfilled. Paula reveals herself to be more than just a judge as she comforts Akelee, and another girl takes off her *American Idol* audition number for good.

Our 30 Contestants

1

9058 Christopher Aaron
23, Atlanta

2

10039 Alexandra Bachelier
20, Miami

3

7675 Christopher Badano
18, New York

4

5061 Natalie Burge
17, Chicago

5

1055 Delano Cagnolatti
23, Los Angeles

6

7420 Khaleef R. Chiles
20, New York

7

10010 Christina Christian
21, Miami

8

2311 Kelly Clarkson
20, Dallas

9

9118 Rodesia Eaves
21, Atlanta

10

1346 Brad Estrin
22, Los Angeles

11

3148 A.J. Gil
17, Seattle

12

7063 Kelli Glover
19, New York

13

9061 Tamyra Gray
22, Atlanta

14

7160 Justin Guarini
23, New York

15

9000 RJ Helton
21, Atlanta

Ain't no mountain high enough for our 30 contestants. But only one will be planting a flag at the top as our American Idol! And maybe the winner will be able to find out what the story is with that silver guy. . . .

16
2053 Adriel Herrera
18, Dallas

17
2088 Kristin Holt
20, Dallas

18
9008 Jamar
22, Atlanta

19
1084 Alexis Lopez
17, Los Angeles

20
7390 Jazmin Lowery
19, New York

21
2070 Nikki McKibbin
23, Dallas

22
5355 Angela J. Peel
20, Chicago

23
3147 Tanesha Ross
24, Seattle

24
9083 Melanie Sanders
22, Atlanta

25
5423 Mark Scott
18, Chicago

26
7667 Gil Sinuet
23, New York

27
1031 Ryan Starr
19, Los Angeles

28
10040 Tenia Taylor
21, Miami

29
5375 Jim Verraros
19, Chicago

30
7294 Justinn Waddell
20, New York

TAMYRA GRAY
"And I Am Telling You, I'm Not Going"

JIM VERRAROS
"When I Fall in Love"

ADRIEL HERRERA
"I'll Be"

Group 1

RODESIA EAVES
"Daydream Believer"

NATALIE BURGE
"Crazy"

BRAD ESTRIN
"Just Once"

RYAN STARR
"Frim Fram Sauce"

CHRISTOPHER AARON
"Still in Love with You"

JUSTINN WADDELL
"When a Man Loves a Woman"

KELLI GLOVER
"I Will Always Love You"

The first 10 contestants compete!

"They sing, you vote, you decide."

The first group of 10 contestants didn't have much time to celebrate their inclusion in the final 30. They arrived in Hollywood and immediately began an intensive music workshop with one of Hollywood's best vocal coaches, Debra Byrd. Hollywood stylist Joanne Lavin of the cool glasses was also available to give advice to the contestants on what to wear for their performance. This set is more upscale than the audition spaces, as we move closer to the fabulous set (with live audience) where

the final 10 will perform. It also includes a new feature: the Red Room, where the contestants hang out and cheer on their fellow singers before and after they perform. Tonight's show starts off with a bang—Simon insults Ryan's shirt. Let the performances begin!

So you want to sound like an American Idol?
Vocal coach Debra Byrd tells you how.

- Your voice will change constantly and you really have to take care of it. You have to take care of what you eat and take care [of] your body and be aware of things that are going on with you; if you have allergies, how foods affect your body, how temperatures affect your body. Be aware of your voice.

- Pick songs that suit you and your voice. Songs are like excellent clothing. You've got that great skirt that fits you so well, or those great pants. Songs are the same way. There was a young lady who was dismissed. She had a lovely voice, but she chose a horrible song. I am sitting in my home looking at her on the show and I'm yelling at the TV, "Sing a different song! Sing a different song!"

- Get a vocal coach. If you don't have one and you aspire for a career in music, get one. It's all dependent upon breathing, it's all dependent on the breath. Get someone to teach you how to breathe.

- Go someplace and sing. Whether it's your church choir, whether it's a community chorus, whether it's a high school choir, a performing arts school, a theater group—go sing.

- Drink lots of water. Drink lots and lots and lots of water.

1. Tamyra Gray, Norcross, GA

Randy: Very good.

Paula: What a brilliant way to start off the show.

Simon: Sensational.

2. Jim Verraros, Crystal Lake, IL

Randy: Kind of boring for me.

Paula: Good job.

Simon: I think if you win this competition we will have failed.

3. Adriel Herrera, Odessa, TX

Paula: Sounded awesome.

Randy: It's the best I've seen you.

Simon: You proved to me and to the others that you are a star.

4. Rodesia Eaves, Columbia, SC

Paula: Great song to sing.

Randy: I loved it, man. Love how you represent that whole urban, gospel-tinge, kind of hip-hop, kind of vibe, kind of thing.

Simon: Oh, dear. I hated your audition.

5. Natalie Burge, Morton, IL

Paula: You're still an awesome performer.

Randy: Overall good.

Simon: I wouldn't know what to do with you as a recording artist based on that song.

6. Brad Estrin, Valley Village, CA

Randy: Dude, I didn't like that.

Paula: I thought you were disconnected from the song.

Simon: Local Chilean karaoke.

7. Ryan Starr, Sunland, CA

Paula: Ryan, you amaze me.

Randy: I was totally thrown off.

Simon: It was very cabaret.

8. Justinn Waddell, Dayton, NJ

Paula: Overall you gave a good performance.

Randy: It's a very interesting outfit to sing that song in.

Simon: You have a great image. It's an interesting one to judge. Mumble mumble.

Paula: He said, "Well done!"

9. Kelli Glover, Cranford, NJ

Randy: It was a terrific choice of song.

Paula: You've been consistently wonderful.

Simon: Stop trying to copy Whitney Houston. That was a karaoke sound-alike performance.

10. Christopher Aaron, Duluth, GA

Randy: You did your thing. You sounded amazing.

Paula: The voice of an angel.

Simon: I don't think you've shone in this competition. Until now.

LIVE!

The Group 1 results show

Tonight is Paula's birthday and our first live results show! Over three million calls were made!

First Chair

Judges' unanimous prediction: Tamyra

Who you chose: **Tamyra Gray!**

Second Chair

Randy and Paula's prediction: Chris

Simon's prediction: Adriel (Though Simon stays with his prediction, he does acknowledge that after reviewing the tapes he thinks Ryan could win herself a chair.)

Who you chose: **Ryan Starr!**

Third Chair

Randy's prediction: Chris
Paula and Simon's prediction: Adriel

Who you chose: ***Jim Verraros!***

ALEXIS LOPEZ
"I Will Survive"

GIL SINUET
"Ribbon in the Sky"

ANGELA PEEL
"Run to You"

Group 2

A.J. GIL
"All or Nothing"

TENIA TAYLOR
"The Greatest Love of All"

ALEXANDRA BACHELIER
"Save the Best for Last"

JAZMIN LOWERY
"You Put a Move on My Heart"

JAMAR
"Careless Whisper"

KELLY CLARKSON
"Respect"

JUSTIN GUARINI
"Ribbon in the Sky"

Group 2 sings for you!

Group 2 has it a little easier than Group 1. They've had an extra week to recuperate from the second round, and they know what to expect—and what mistakes not to make—after watching Group 1! In addition to working with Debra and Joanne, they also have time to hit the town and greet their fans. Is Tenia really signing that guy's back?

Group 2 also gets some counseling to help deal with the stress of performing, competing, homesickness, and Simon. The guys have come up with one way to cope: They throw darts at a picture of Simon on a dartboard. Whatever works for you.

Look like an American Idol with stylist Joanne Lavin's fashion tips:

- **Fashion always recycles. You can find great buys in secondhand and thrift stores.**
- **Don't be afraid to be creative—fashion ideas can come from anywhere.**
- **You can always change your look with accessories and not spend a lot of money.**

Bottom Line: It's not really about money as much as it is about creativity—it's about having your own style.

1. Alexis Lopez, Modesto, CA

Randy: You've definitely grown.

Paula: You've come out of your shell.

Simon: I wish you hadn't sung that song. It sounds like karaoke. I hate karaoke.

2. Gil Sinuet, Garfield, NJ

Paula: I think this is your best performance.

Randy: I liked the way you did that little curl thing at the end.

Simon: I don't think you look like the American Idol, but I think you sound like the American Idol.

3. Angela Peel, Chicago, IL

Randy: That was very good. You chose a very tough song. I mean, Whitney is one of the American Idols.

Paula: You really shined.

Simon: You didn't do karaoke. You're so tall I wouldn't criticize you anyway. Fantastic.

4. A.J. Gil, Tacoma, WA

Randy: I think I've seen you better.

Paula: I've seen better performances. Lack of energy.

Simon: I think you have a nice voice. I thought the laugh in the middle was hideous—and the shirt. I think you've blown it, but then I got it wrong last week.

5. Tenia Taylor, Miami, FL

Paula: You look stunning. Tough song to sing. You started off shaky but connected halfway through.

Randy: Wow, man. I was waiting to see those shorts. Where are the shorts?

Simon: I don't think you're that good. I don't think the outfit worked and I don't think you pulled off the song.

6. Alexandra Bachelier, Miami, FL

Randy: That was definitely Miami karaoke to me.

Paula: The talent is just getting so superior.

Simon: Save the best for last. You didn't. It wasn't good enough.

7. Jazmin Lowery, Hempstead, NY

Paula: This is a difficult song to sing, and you certainly pulled it off—beautiful voice.

Randy: I didn't think that was very good, actually, at all.

Simon: I thought it was brilliant. What I love about you is I know you're nervous but you're real. I think you have a beautiful voice.

8. Jamar, Atlanta, GA

Randy: Jamar, man, I think I've seen you much better than this.

Paula: I'm not crazy about the song selection. The key was a little too high for you.

Simon: You didn't sing it, you shouted it.

9. Kelly Clarkson, Joshua, TX

Randy: Kelly, Kelly, Kelly. Very, very, very, very good.

Paula: When it ain't broke, don't fix it.

Simon: You have a good voice but I couldn't remember you from the previous rounds.

10. Justin Guarini, Doylestown, PA

Paula: You gave it some quiet sincerity and I really, really enjoyed your performance.

Randy: I don't know if it was amazing for me. In Pasadena you blew me away.

Simon: I think Gil sang it better except you have something . . . and it's called the X factor. What is it? Well, it's very simple. It's you.

LIVE!

The Group 2 results show

Over 6.9 million calls were made for the favorites

in the second group!

First Chair

Judges' unanimous prediction: Justin

Who you chose: **Justin Guarini!**

Second Chair

Randy's prediction: Angela
Paula's prediction: Alexis
Simon's prediction: Gil, but changes his prediction to Alexis on the live show.

Who you chose: **Kelly Clarkson!**

Third Chair

Judges' unanimous prediction: Alexis

Who you chose: **A.J. Gil!**

RJ HELTON
"I'll Be There"

KRISTIN HOLT
"Fallin'"

MARK SCOTT
"My Girl"

Group 3

NIKKI MCKIBBIN
"Total Eclipse of the Heart"

CHRISTOPHER BADANO
"I Swear"

MELANIE SANDERS
"And I Am Telling You, I'm Not Going"

EJAY DAY
"I'll Be"

TANESHA ROSS
"Until You Come Back to Me
That's What I'm Gonna Do"

KHALEEF CHILES
"My Cherie Amour"

CHRISTINA CHRISTIAN
"At Last"

Group 3 faces the judges!

Group 3 had a tumultuous week. It seems Delano Cagnolatti is not 23, as he claimed on his application, but 29! Since the rules clearly state that participants must be between the ages of 16 and 24, Delano was disqualified. We actually thought he didn't look a day over 19! Alternate EJay Day —not to be confused with RJ or A.J.—got the call to take Delano's place and booked a ticket on the next flight from Georgia. The Delano incident behind them, Group 3 was ready to face the judges. . . .

A Note from Paula

My advice has always been the same. First you have to be brutally honest with yourself. Ask yourself these questions: "Am I really truly talented enough to make it in this profession? Do I possess an undying passion that will never waver? Do I have the drive to keep on trying no matter how much rejection I may face?" If you can answer all of these questions with a yes, then be true to your heart and go for it! Having said that, be wise enough to set a realistic time frame to achieve your goals. If at that time you have not accomplished what you set out to, it may be time to explore another path. You never know, you may achieve greatness where you least expected to. Good luck, stay grounded, and never stop dreaming.

XOXO Paula

1. RJ Helton, Cumming, GA

Randy: RJ, love those initials, man, those happen to be my initials as well. You did very well man, very good.

Paula: You gave a solid performance.

Simon: I could not disagree with you more, Paula. I did not think that was solid. Seriously, we have to get this competition back on track. In the last two episodes, two losers have been voted through for one reason and one reason only—it was the sympathy vote.

2. Kristin Holt, Plano, TX

Paula: I enjoyed your performance better when I first saw it in Dallas.

Randy: We are trying to find the best in America. I didn't think you were anywhere close to that tonight.

Simon: If I were judging a beauty competition, you'd win. But we're judging a singing competition. You're out of your league in this.

3. Mark Scott, Portage, IN

Paula: I fought for you in Chicago. I love your voice but I didn't care for the song choice.

Randy: Wasn't good tonight, dude.

Simon: What did you think?

4. Nikki McKibbin, Grand Prairie, TX

Randy: You did your thing. I like the kind of edge.

Paula: I've always admired the fact that you kind of march to the beat of your own drum. I love your voice.

Simon: I think you are one of the strongest contestants in this competition because you have originality, and I think this is what this competition should be about.

5. Chris Badano, Parsippany, NJ

Paula: You did a great job; however, I'm not blown away by your choice of song.

Randy: What happened to all that rah-rah energy you had, dude? You were like the life of the party.

Simon: You're a good-looking boy. Young girls will love you. I thought your singing voice was average.

6. Melanie Sanders, Vicksburg, MS

Randy: You were really good tonight.

Paula: You did a great job. Good for you.

Simon: You're a beautiful-looking girl. You sang it well. I can't help but think cabaret, though.

7. EJay Day, Lawrenceville, GA

Simon: No one has sung better than that today. You sang your heart out.

Paula: You've blown everyone away.

Randy: I didn't even know you had that kind of vocal range. You were incredible.

8. Tanesha Ross, Auburn, WA

Paula: Your voice is really pure and beautiful. You don't need to do so many vocal runs.

Randy: To me, you just never found the note. Today was not good.

Simon: I would say you didn't shine like a star and I'd say so what? There are just better people.

9. Khaleef Chiles, Plainfield, NJ

Randy: You look petrified. I thought it was just okay.

Paula: I think you took the song and you made it yours. Your voice sounded excellent.

Simon: You are someone who cares about you. Good luck, hope you win the competition.

10. Christina Christian, Miami, FL

Paula: You have such star presence. The camera loves you.

Randy: I agree with Paula. Interesting choice of song coming from you.

Simon: Thank God for you. I thought you were fantastic. I loved it.

LIVE!

The Group 3 results show

Are you tall enough to ride this emotional roller coaster?

Last night millions of votes were cast and many tears were shed onscreen. In addition to announcing the results, tonight's show is spent addressing what happened. Let's see, Delano was disqualified, EJay arrived to take his place, Simon crossed the line, Randy had his fill, RJ was caught in the middle, and all the contestants, but especially Kristin and Tanesha, handled themselves incredibly well in the face of enormous pressure. Can *you* imagine going out there to face the judges after that? Tonight, Simon concedes that *loser* may have been a bad choice of words and revises his statement to say that he does not believe, based on talent, that A.J. and Jim deserve to be in the final 10. Well, we'll just have to wait and see about that!

First Chair

Who you chose: **Christina Christian!**

Second Chair

Who you chose: *Nikki McKibbin!*

Third Chair

Judges' predictions:
Simon: No comment. (That's a first!)
Paula: EJay
Randy: EJay

Who you chose:

EJay Day!

The Wild-Card Show!

The first nine finalists were chosen by you, the viewers at home, but the tenth wild-card finalist was chosen by our panel of judges. Randy, Simon, and Paula narrowed the talented field of 21 down to just 5—Kelli Glover, Christopher Aaron, Alexis Lopez, RJ Helton, and Angela Peel—and asked them to come back to perform another song. While Randy feels that all five can really sing, and Paula calls the group truly gifted, Simon whines that they are not all his favorites!

The judges deliberate and agree that they will be selecting the wild card based not only on tonight but on overall performance. How can they possibly choose just one? They must, and they do. The decision is unanimous: RJ Helton, who just one week ago was caught in the middle of Randy and Simon's verbal joust, will be the tenth finalist!

Our 10 Finalists

Tamyra

Tamyra Gray was a pre-K teacher in Atlanta before auditioning for *American Idol.* The 22-year-old enjoyed working with kids. "When children know that you're serious with them, that you're not playing, then they listen to you." Tamyra's got us listening, too.

What has your experience on American Idol *been like?* *American Idol* for me is like artist development. It's artist development without having to pay for it. You get to go through everything that any performer needs to experience before they become an artist. The only thing is, you're actually doing it. It's not pretend. You're really

doing it. I'm loving it because it's one big learning lesson.

Best thing? Every moment is a highlight.

Worst thing? There hasn't been any bad. The only thing that hurts is when you have friends who get hurt.

How are the other contestants? Is it really as support-ive as it looks on TV? It's really great to be in a competition where it's not a harsh competition but a friendly competition, where you're able to support people and people are supporting you, and you have a shoulder to cry on should you need to cry on it. We all want to see each other's dreams come true.

You and Chris were already friends? We knew each other through some mutual friends in Atlanta. I went to the audi-tion and he was, like, five people ahead of me. From that moment on, we were together. We could hang together through the entire competition and that was the best thing.

Do you do anything special before you perform? I say a prayer. A prayer for strength. A prayer that my vocals meet expectations and that I have a good time and enjoy my performance and really show people that this is what I want to do.

What does your family think about all this? I'm still Tamyra. They've been through the struggle with me. And everybody's just so happy to see things finally coming together.

Do you read the message boards? The sad thing is, I wish I could just say thank you to all of the people who are supporting me, because I had a girl who wrote in and said that she was having a baby and she was naming her baby after me. I've had the crazy marriage proposal things. And then I had this one that really touched me and it really brought me to tears. It was a girl named China who lives in Tennessee. She was saying that she wanted to audition for it, but for whatever reason, she couldn't get there. And she was saying that I reminded her of herself, and that regardless of what happens, "Know that you are a star in somebody's eyes."

Anything you would change about your experience on American Idol? I wouldn't change anything. I wouldn't ask for a different set of judges. I wouldn't ask for a different set of contestants. This is the way it's sup-posed to be.

If you could be anyone for a day who would it be? I'd be me!

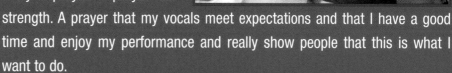

Ryan

It's hard to believe that *American Idol* was 19-year-old Ryan Starr's first audition! Ryan, from Sunland, CA, has modeled, coached swimming, and worked at a designer clothing store. "I'm just a regular girl who's a singer," she says. "I'm a total dork in real life."

Surprises? The whole thing is actually a surprise to me because when I first went to the first audition, I went with a friend just because I wanted to practice. My first audition was going to be that Monday for a movie I wanted to be in, and I was singing in the movie. So I went to the audition for *American Idol* for practice. I didn't really go because I thought I would make it. And I think making it to the top 10 was probably the biggest surprise of my life. I wasn't prepared for that at all. There was no way in my wildest imagination I thought I would be the second person.

Best thing? The auditions. The actual performances. I've never really been in front of a judge and under that much pressure. And I've never learned so much, so fast. I've learned, I think, almost everything I'd need to know about showcasing to any kind of record label I could think of, or any kind of judge, for that matter. I'm more confident now. I know what I need to work on and I know what I lack and what I want to have, but don't have yet. And I know how to take criticism better now. I've always been kind of like the Ugly Duckling. All my friends went to college and I turned down college to be a singer, so it's been cool to be around people who are like that. I like that a lot.

Worst thing? Not having been used to going through auditions before. I'm not used to seeing people lose. Physically, too, it's just straining on the body. I don't get a lot of sleep. My appetite is just in chaos. And your emotions are just like up and down, up and down, up and down. People are getting dropped, people are crying, your close friends are leaving, and your close friends are coming back. You're like, "I can't take this!"

On her group: Our group was really close outside of the filming. We didn't do any on-camera stuff, but we went out to clubs together; we went to the beach together; we went shopping together. The other groups didn't have cars. Two people in our group have cars, so we got to actually do stuff.

If you could be anyone for a day who would it be? I'd sort of want to see what it's like to be my mom.

What does your family think of all this? I kind of excelled in high school. I got accepted to a college, but I turned it down so that I could sing. So I think that my family's never really supported my musical career. Before this, they didn't support it. Now that I'm on TV, they think it's cool. They support me now.

Have any people from your past come out of the woodwork? Of course, all the guys I dated: "Oh hey, how've you been?" Even the guys who dumped me. I had a guy who dumped me call me and he was like, "Hey, let's go out. Let's get coffee." And I'm like, "Yeah, right! You dumped me and broke my heart!"

Do you read the message boards? It's like a high school reunion on my message board.

Anything you'd like to say to your fans? I'd just want them to know that I'm a down-to-earth tomboy and I really don't think anything's more important than the music. I don't want the world to know me as a girl who makes her own clothes; I want them to know me as a dorky tomboy, because that's who I am.

Favorite Album: *A compilation CD of my own including Pat Benatar, Janet, Jars of Clay (my favorite band), and Gipsy Kings*

Favorite Male Pop Artist: *Girls rule but if I have to choose I would say Usher.*

Favorite Female Pop Artist: *Janet Jackson*

Favorite Performer: *Madonna*

Favorite Singer of All Time: *Celine Dion*

Who are your American Idols? *Madonna, because she has outstanding longevity and she always seems to know just what to do next. Pat Benatar. She is one of the few women who made a place for women in a man's rock world. The Beatles. They made the hits.*

Jim

A month and a half ago Jim Verraros auditioned for *American Idol* after a class at Chicago's Columbia College, where the 19-year-old just finished his first year. "I just figured I'd mosey on down and give it a shot. And look where I am. It's just unbelievable."

What has your experience on American Idol *been like?* It's been amazing. It's been nerve-wracking. It's been a big emotional roller coaster. The longer you wait, the more your mind starts to wander, the more you think, "Oh God, am I going to make it?" But the people you meet make it all worth it.

Is it really as supportive as it looks on TV? It's totally real. It was never planned. It was never asked for.

Surprises? To make top 10. I was shocked, extremely shocked, but honored. I never knew people would recognize me. It's weird to say, but I've never been so loved and hated in my entire life.

On the message boards: It's just unbelievable. If people knew me, would they be saying the same stuff? I think you definitely have to keep an open mind about it. For every bad comment, you get three supporters.

What does your family think about all this? They're very happy because they know how much I've wanted this. Of course they're a tad skeptical because we've spent quite a bit of money on clothes, trying to look good on camera. I'm hoping this will take me somewhere, that I'll be able to pay them back.

On the whole image thing: In this day and age—and I hate to say this, but it's so true—if Aretha Franklin were her same body type and she were my age, would she have gotten this far in a competition like this? If I were the 70 pounds heavier that I was, would I have gotten as far in this competition?

Any advice to others on how to get in shape? If you want it bad enough, you'll do it.

Has anyone from your past come out of the woodwork? Honestly, after this competition, you figure out who your true friends are, and who's been there for you all the way and who's known you before this whole thing started.

If you could be anyone for a day who would it be? I think I'd want to be Elton John for a day. Simply because he is the epitome of inventiveness—or re-inventiveness, I should say. He has made huge strides in his career. Having to overcome his sexuality and still making a positive name for himself, regardless of all the stereotypes—I think that's amazing. I think that he is one of the most talented performers I've ever heard. He's just a great, great person in the music business.

Favorite Album: Room for Squares, *John Mayer*

Favorite Male Pop Artist: *Elton John*

Favorite Female Pop Artist: *Janet Damita Jo Jackson*

Favorite Performer: **NSYNC*

Favorite Singer of All Time: *Celine Dion*

Who are your American Idols? *Wow, that's a really hard question to answer. I would have to say Janet Jackson, Madonna, Elton John, U2, Craig David, Alicia Keys, Nelly Furtado. Basically anyone who's inventive and has been able to withstand the constant changes of the music business. And someone who's different, as well. Being different is something that's recently been embraced in the music business, and difference is always a good thing.*

Justin

Justin Guarini had a good feeling about *American Idol.* And he was right. It's turned out well for the 23-year-old from Doylestown, PA. Simon said Justin was what he meant when he used the term "X factor," and Paula was moved to tears by Justin's performance in Hollywood. American Idol or not, we'll be hearing about Justin Guarini.

What has your experience on American Idol been like? It's been a roller coaster ride. It's been just awesome. It's unbelievable. I think the best part of it's been the other contestants.

Favorite Album: Thriller, *Michael Jackson*

Favorite Male Pop Artist: *Elton John*

Favorite Female Pop Artist: *Whitney Houston*

Favorite Performer: *Michael Jackson*

Favorite Singer of All Time: *Stevie Wonder*

Who are your American Idols? *My parents, Sidney Poitier, Quincy Jones, Stevie Wonder*

They've been such a refreshing atmosphere. We're all in the same boat; we're all lucky kids; and we're so supportive of one another. And that is something that you never see in any sort of audition process or, really, a competition.

Is it really as supportive as it looks on TV? It's hard to believe. But we really have all been together and we're just getting tighter and tighter. Simon was a little shocked by how much we all gelled. He's like, "You guys are competitors and you should hate one another." And I think he almost wants to see us being catty and in-fighting. And that's just not the way this group of kids are—at all.

Surprises? The production aspect. That's really surprising to me. I've never been exposed to television production. I've always watched it, but I've never been in it.

Worst thing? Being so far from my friends and family and having to adjust to a completely different lifestyle. I do have family out here, but my closest friends are back home.

What does your family think about all this? They have always supported me 100 percent.

Have you become close friends with any of the other contestants? We're all out of our element, so we really band together. It's almost like those old covered wagons circling up to protect one another. We all watch each other's backs.

Do you do anything special before you perform? No, I really just relax.

If you could be anyone for a day who would it be? I would be a Zen monk.

Do you read the message boards? I think the message boards are a great place to exchange ideas and to make friends, but I tend to stay away from them completely because I'm focusing on what I'm doing. I value the American public's opinion, but I don't let it define who I am.

How does it feel to be making Paula swoon? It's an honor! She has opened her heart and allowed me to touch her. It's an honor to be able to touch someone in her position.

Anything for fans? My advice to everyone is, do what you want. Search your heart and find out what you really love to do and do it. Do it no matter what.

Kelly

Kelly Clarkson deserves our R-E-S-P-E-C-T. The day this 20-year-old from Joshua, TX, moved back home from L.A., her friend Jessica told her about the *American Idol* auditions in Dallas. She tried out the next day.

What has your experience on American Idol *been like? Any surprises?* It's all surprising. It's an audition, but it's more like preparing me with media. It's showing me how everything's going to change, so I'll be prepared when it does. I'm getting experience with everything and not having to pay for it.

Best thing? Nobody really knew me, and when they heard me sing, it was kind of flattering, because that's all people knew. They couldn't go on anything else. All they could go on was my performance.

Worst thing? The worst thing is seeing that talent and seeing it not being able to advance.

What does your family think about all this? A lot of my family didn't

know I could sing this well. My family is all spread out. They're in Alaska, California, North Carolina—they're all over. They all saw me perform and they called my mom that night and I was flipping out. And they had a big party when I got home.

Do you read the message boards? Of course I read them, because people take their time. People take the time to write it. Most of them say, "Kelly, please read," and I want to respond. Me and Tamyra were talking about that earlier: We want to respond to them, and we want to talk to them, but we're not allowed to. I read the good and the bad. The thing is, the bad rolls off my back.

On movies: My first job was at a movie theater. I worked there for two years. I was 16 and I worked until I graduated, and then I moved out and moved on. One of my girlfriends is still putting herself through college at that job and she's a manager there. And I still preview the movies before anybody sees them. I'm a movie freak! All my friends can't believe why I just don't go into acting. I actually write scripts. I'm more into behind-the-scenes kind of stuff. I've written two movies and have people looking at them.

If you could be anyone for a day who would it be? I adore Reba McEntire! I'm such a country girl when it comes to that. I love her, ever since I was a little girl. She's so talented. She does management, she's a businesswoman, she does singing, she does acting, she does theater.

Anything you want to say to your fans? Don't believe everything you see and hear. That's for anybody in this industry. You've got to remember that it's a TV show and they're going to do stuff for ratings. And I'm okay with that because I'm getting exposure, I'm getting mad exposure. I'm getting stuff I couldn't pay for.

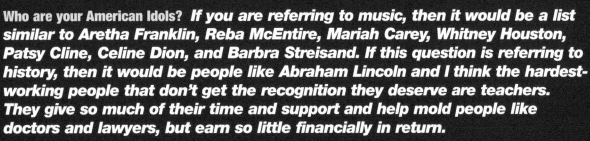

Favorite Album: **Jagged Little Pill,** *Alanis Morrissette*

Favorite Male Pop Artist: *Ever since I was a little girl I have loved listening to Michael Bolton.*

Favorite Female Pop Artist: *It's a tie between Mariah Carey and Whitney Houston.*

Favorite Performer: *It's a tie between Steven Tyler from Aerosmith and Gwen Stefani from No Doubt.*

Favorite Singer of All Time: *Reba McEntire*

Who are your American Idols? *If you are referring to music, then it would be a list similar to Aretha Franklin, Reba McEntire, Mariah Carey, Whitney Houston, Patsy Cline, Celine Dion, and Barbra Streisand. If this question is referring to history, then it would be people like Abraham Lincoln and I think the hardest-working people that don't get the recognition they deserve are teachers. They give so much of their time and support and help mold people like doctors and lawyers, but earn so little financially in return.*

A.J.

Eighteen-year-old high school junior A.J. Gil from Tacoma, WA, will be heading back to school if he doesn't make it on *American Idol*. With his boyish good looks, Backstreet name/facial hair, and rendition of "The Star-Spangled Banner," it's no wonder he slipped into the final 10.

What has your experience on American Idol *been like?* It's just a very good experience. I feel privileged.

Any surprises? I didn't expect to get this far.

Best thing? The exposure is a good thing, but also, just experiencing this whole *American Idol* situation because I've never been through this kind of thing.

Worst thing? Losing the friends who didn't make it. Saying bye to them is kinda hard.

How are the other contestants? We do everything natural. What we show on TV is how we feel toward the other contestants.

What does your family think about all this? My mom is very proud; my dad, he's just kind of on the quiet side.

Has anyone from your past come out of the woodwork? Just a lot of friends. A lot of people who didn't really like me—now they're

calling me and saying, "What's up? How's it going?" And of course, I'm going to say, "What's up?" Because I don't hate anybody and I don't have any remorse toward nobody; I'm trying to be everybody's friend. And if they show me their good face, then I guess I'm going to be nice.

Would you do American Idol *again? Anything you'd do differently?* I would do it again. But I would change my performance—project more and show more expression.

Do you do anything special before you perform? I pray.

Celebrity sightings: I saw Nick Carter. He was staying in my hotel. He recognized me. He was like, "Do I know you from somewhere?" and I was like, "I don't think so. Maybe *American Idol*." And he was like, "Oh yeah!"

What will you buy with your first million? I want to buy my mom a house and a car.

If you could be anyone for a day who would it be? I would be Puff Daddy. P-Diddy. Yeah.

Favorite Album: **Black and Blue,** *Backstreet Boys*

Favorite Male Pop Artist: *Stevie Wonder*

Favorite Female Pop Artist: *Mariah Carey*

Favorite Performer: *Usher*

Favorite Singer of All Time: *Brian McKnight*

Who are your American Idols? **NSYNC, Usher, Brian McKnight, Brandy, Tyrese*

Christina

wenty-one-year-old Christina Christian just finished her junior year at the University of Florida in Gainesville. "No matter what I'm going to finish here in college, whether it be by night or correspondence, the school said they'd work with me." We suspect Christina might have to take advantage of those correspondence courses.

What has your experience on American Idol *been like?* It's a lot tougher now and definitely scarier going in.

Tougher now? Oh yeah.

Best thing? I think just the people I've gotten to meet. Even the judges: They're all very, very nice. All the people who are involved with doing the show, all the talent that's on the show. Just the relationships that we've made—that's the best thing.

Worst thing? Being away from my family. That's been pretty tough.

What was it like being there for the judge fight? Going through all that—it really honestly did affect a lot of people. After that show was taped, we saw people kind of seclude themselves for a little bit. It really did hurt a lot of people. It hurt us, so the people who got good comments couldn't really enjoy the good comments because we were so worried about our friends.

Favorite Album: **The Velvet Rope,** *Janet Jackson*

Favorite Male Pop Artists: *Michael Jackson, George Michael, Justin Timberlake*

Favorite Female Pop Artists: *Madonna, Janet Jackson, Britney Spears*

Favorite Performer: *Janet Jackson*

Favorite Singer of All Time: *Celine Dion*

Who are your American Idols? *Janet Jackson, Michael Jackson, Madonna, Britney Spears, Justin Timberlake*

You don't think that you're going to get the chair. I was completely shocked. Completely.

Best thing? Just meeting the people and just getting that experience and the whole attention and exposure. Generally, it's been great.

Worst thing? I guess just the emotional thing, having to go through that, and the criticism and having to deal with it. Just dealing with it and accepting it—that's been the worst thing for me.

How are the other contestants? The majority of the people were very cool, they were very supportive. Especially Melanie: She's one of my friends from Atlanta. She was very excited and very happy for me. She was just there for me the whole time.

Do you do anything special before you perform? Just prayer, basically. I'm not one of those knock-on-wood types of guys, I guess.

Do you read the message boards? Unfortunately, I do. I hate it, but I do. It's hard. I just try to let it go and throw it off my shoulders and just say, "Moving right along."

If you could be anyone for a day who would it be? Justin Timberlake.

Anything you'd like to say to your fans? Thanks to my family and friends; the people at Six Flags; the people at Royal Caribbean; the people I've worked with everywhere; and the people who are voting for me.

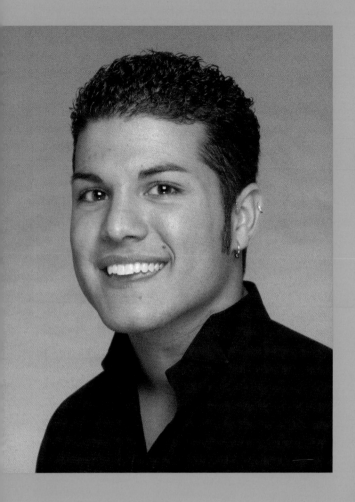

RJ

Originally wild-card RJ Helton didn't want to come back to be on the wild-card show. Twenty-one-year-old RJ, from Cumming, GA, was the unfortunate innocent contestant caught in Randy and Simon's crossfire. "I don't feel like coming back to be cut down again. If that's going to be the case, don't bother, I don't want to do it," RJ said. Luckily for his fans, who include Randy, he took the second chance.

What has your experience on American Idol been like? It's been very emotional—the worst and best experience of my life.

Any surprises? Making that tenth spot.

On the fight: It was definitely the most dramatic show by far. It was just an emotional week for us: We were up and we were down, and we were up and let down, and it just made it really difficult for us to focus. It just was what it was.

Worst thing? Even above [the judge fight], the worst thing has been watching friends you've gotten close to be cut down, get crushed.

Is it more competitive now that it's the finals? We're still tight. Everyone is so supportive of one another. We're all in the same boat.

Favorite Album: **Daydream, *Mariah Carey***

Favorite Male Pop Artist: ***Brian McKnight***

Favorite Female Pop Artist: ***Mariah Carey***

Favorite Performer: ***Janet Jackson***

Favorite Singer of All Time: ***Mariah Carey***

Who are your American Idols? *I only have one. My mother. She is a woman of great integrity, honesty, and love. She has the strength of an army and is not only my mother but my greatest friend.*

Do you do anything special before you perform? I pray a lot. I meditate. I speak to my grandmother, basically, and to God and ask for the strength. And ask for God to sing through me because it's His voice.

What does your family think about all this? They're very excited. It is so different for me to go back home, because I'm very grounded. So I wanted to go back home and have my mom just hold me, I haven't seen her in so long. It's kind of hard going home because people go, "You're a star," and I'm like, "No, I'm Christina."

Do you read the message boards? Really, honestly, what makes me feel good is my family; what makes me feel good is knowing that the judges like me; and that the American public likes me enough to vote for me.

If you could be anyone for a day who would it be? I'd want to be Simon!

Anything you'd like your fans to know? Hopefully, they see that I'm honestly a very caring person. As all my friends know, I've helped so many people out and I don't look for anything in return, and I'm here just to give back.

Would you do American Idol *again?* Yeah.

Would you do anything differently? No. I like the way it's been going.

Favorite Album: Let's Talk About Love, *Celine Dion*

Favorite Male Pop Artist: *Usher*

Favorite Female Pop Artist: *Celine Dion*

Favorite Performer: *Celine Dion*

Favorite Singer of All Time: *Celine Dion*

Who are your American Idols? *My mother, Celine Dion, Rosa Parks*

Nikki

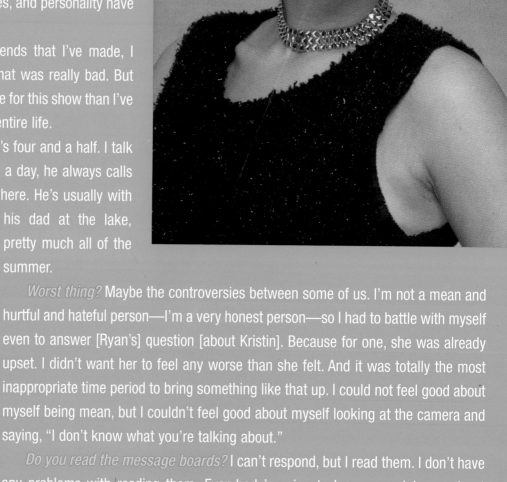

Back in Grand Prairie, TX, 23-three-year-old Nikki McKibbin owns her own karaoke company, Angel Fire Productions. Nikki says that as a Libra she likes to be the center of attention. Her unique look, song choices, and personality have certainly got ours!

Best thing? The friends that I've made, I think. I hate flying, so that was really bad. But I've been on a plane more for this show than I've ever been in my whole entire life.

You have a son? He's four and a half. I talk with him a million times a day, he always calls me, so it feels like he's here. He's usually with his dad at the lake, pretty much all of the summer.

Worst thing? Maybe the controversies between some of us. I'm not a mean and hurtful and hateful person—I'm a very honest person—so I had to battle with myself even to answer [Ryan's] question [about Kristin]. Because for one, she was already upset. I didn't want her to feel any worse than she felt. And it was totally the most inappropriate time period to bring something like that up. I could not feel good about myself being mean, but I couldn't feel good about myself looking at the camera and saying, "I don't know what you're talking about."

Do you read the message boards? I can't respond, but I read them. I don't have any problems with reading them. Everybody's going to have an opinion, and not

everybody's opinion is going to be good, and not everybody's opinion is going to be the same. I'm getting poems and marriage proposals. It's very inspiring, if you're in a bad mood.

Have you become close friends with any of the other contestants? Out of my 10, I would have to say RJ is my best friend. We were absolutely just meant to click right from the beginning. He's great.

What is your favorite karaoke song to sing? I love to do "Stand Back" by Stevie Nicks. And I also love to do "Forgiven" by Alanis Morrissette.

If you could be anyone for a day who would it be? That would be Nikki Giovanni. Only because she's my favorite poet and she seems to be somebody who knows so much, and she has so much inspiration and so much love behind everything she writes.

On her look: I don't see the "uniqueness" and "originality." What I see about myself is that I try to be bold and I try to catch people's attention. I change my style constantly. I think that the reason that is being brought up so much is that I stand out in the group. It's not that I'm claiming to be unique and original. I just claim to be me.

Anything you would change about this experience? No, just because I think I've been true to myself. When I got here to do this, I said, "I'm not changing my hair color. This is me and this is how I am and this is how I've

been. I'm not going to change the way that I dress. I'm not going to change anything about myself. I'm just going to go and I'm going to be me. Hopefully, they'll love me and if they don't, they don't. At least I was being true to me."

Favorite Male Pop Artist: *Michael Jackson*

Favorite Female Pop Artists: *Janet Jackson, Madonna*

Favorite Performer: *Janet Jackson*

Who are your American Idols? *Celebrity-wise, Stevie Nicks. She is so talented. Otherwise, my parents. They are both great.*

EJay

wenty-year-old comeback kid EJay Day made it to the final 45 in Hollywood before getting cut and heading home to Lawrenceville, GA. But when Delano was disqualified, EJay jumped back on a plane, blew everyone away, and moved from alternate to finalist.

What has your experience on American Idol *been like?* It's the biggest roller coaster ride I've ever been on. Different emotions. Everything's going on all at once. It's very overwhelming, but still, I'm having a great time.

What was it like to get that call to come back? I freaked out. I was at Six Flags at work, and my message was going off—I have a ringer—so it was ringing and I checked it. Somebody made a joke like, "I bet you it's *American Idol.*" And I'm like, "Yeah, sure it is." So I checked it and I was out in front of everybody, and all of a sud-

den I just started crying and I was overwhelmed. And everybody was like, "Are you okay? What happened?" And I'm like, "It's *American Idol.*" And they're like, "What are you talking about?" And I'm like, "It's *American Idol,* oh my gosh!" Everybody just freaked out. And so I had to leave and had 45 minutes to pack and get on the plane. It was pretty chaotic. That's when everything started.

Any (other) surprises? I wasn't expecting to get actually picked in the top 10, so that was the biggest shocker.

Best thing? The friendships that I've made with each of the contestants.

Do you do anything special before you perform? My ritual is to pray, obviously, and to call my mom.

What does your family think about all this? They never pushed me. They've always let me do my own thing.

Do you read the message boards? Every once in a while, I'll see how many are posted. I try to stay away from that just to keep my focus right.

On his fellow potential wild cards: The five of us decided we were gonna have a party together. We put all differences aside and really got along for the night.

Anything you'd like to say to your fans? If you have a dream and a goal, whatever it be, don't give up on it and don't let anyone tell you that you can't do it. And if anyone does tell you that, let that be incentive to work even harder. Stand up for what you believe and don't compromise yourself.

If you could be anyone for a day who would it be? Lenny Kravitz. He's such a unique person. He's so talented. He's got lots of different things going on in his head. I'd love to have his brain for a day.

Would you do it again? I'm definitely glad I did it. No regrets at all.

Anything you'd do differently? Everything happened for a reason.

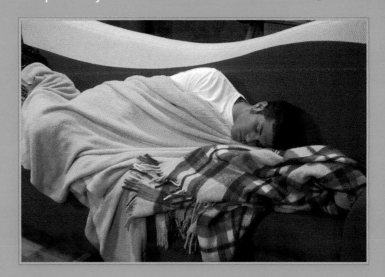

You Be the Judge!

Official Sweepstakes Rules & Regulations

One of these 8 finalists will be the American Idol. Stay tuned and vote!

I. HOW TO ENTER

NO PURCHASE NECESSARY. Enter by mailing your name, address, phone number, and date of birth to: American Idol "You Be the Judge" Sweepstakes, Random House Children's Books, 1540 Broadway, 19th floor, New York, NY 10036. Entries must be mailed separately and received by Random House no later than November 1, 2002. LIMIT ONE ENTRY PER PERSON. Partially completed or illegible entries will not be accepted. Random House is not responsible for lost, late, mutilated, illegible, stolen, postage due, incomplete or misdirected entries.

II. ELIGIBILITY

Sweepstakes is open to all legal residents of the United States, excluding Puerto Rico, who are between the ages of 16 and 24 as of December 1, 2002. All federal, state and local laws and regulations apply. Void wherever prohibited or restricted by law. Employees, officers, directors, agents, and representatives of Sponsor, Fox Broadcasting Company, American Idol Productions, Inc., FremantleMedia North America, Inc., Microsoft Corporation, 19 Entertainment Limited, Fox Group, Inc. and each of their respective parent companies, subsidiaries and affiliates, members of their immediate families (parents, children, siblings, spouses) and persons living in the same household of such persons (whether related or not) are not eligible to enter this sweepstakes.

III. PRIZES

There will be one (1) Grand Prize Winner, ten (10) first prize winners, ten (10) second prize winners and ten (10) third prize winners selected. One Grand Prize (1) winner will win a trip to the closest audition city to their permanent residence, including round trip airfare and a one night hotel stay for two people, and sit in with the judges and participate in the judging process as a consultant during the first series of auditions for the 2nd series of *American Idol* (approximate retail value $1,500.00 US). If the winner is under 18 years of age, the second person traveling must be a legal parent or guardian. Travel and use of accommodation are at risk of Winner and Winner's parent/legal guardian and Random House, Inc., FremantleMedia, their parents, affiliates and subsidiaries do not assume any liability. Ten (10) first prize winners will receive an autographed compilation CD from the 10 finalists from the 1st season of *American Idol* (approximate retail value $20 US each). Ten (10) 2nd prize winners will receive an autographed copy of the official book "American Idol: The Search for a Superstar" from Bantam Books (approximate retail value $10 US each). Ten (10) 3rd prize winners will receive a one year subscription to YM magazine (approximate retail value $12 US each). If for any reason prizes are not available or cannot be fulfilled, Random House, Inc., reserves the right to substitute a prize of equal or greater value, including, but not limited to, cash equivalent. Taxes, if any, are the Winner's sole responsibility. Prizes are not transferable and cannot be assigned. No prize or cash substitutes allowed, except at the discretion of the sponsor due to prize availability as set forth above.

IV. WINNERS

Odds of winning depend on the total number of entries received. Winners will be selected in a random drawing on or about November 15, 2002 from all eligible entries received by Random House Children's Books. By participating, entrants agree to be bound by the Official Rules and the decision of the judges, which shall be final and binding in all respects. All prizes will be awarded in the name of the winner, or if the winner is under the age of 18, in the name of the winner's parent or guardian. Winner, or winner's parent or legal guardian will be notified by mail and winner and winner's parent/legal guardian will be required to sign and return affidavit(s) of eligibility and release of liability within 14 days of notification. A noncompliance within that time period or the return of any notification as undeliverable will result in disqualification and the selection of an alternate winner. In the event of any other noncompliance with rules and conditions, prize may be awarded to an alternate winner. Winners will be notified by mail on or about November 20, 2002. Taxes, if any, are the winner's sole responsibility.

V. RESERVATIONS

By participating, winner (and winner's parent/legal guardian) agrees that Sponsor, Fox Broadcasting Company, American Idol Productions, Inc., FremantleMedia North America, Inc., Microsoft Corporation, 19 Entertainment Limited, Fox Group, Inc., its parent companies, assigns, subsidiaries or affiliates, and advertising, promotion and fulfillment agencies will have no liability whatsoever, and will be held harmless by winner (and winner's parent/legal guardian) for any liability for any injuries, losses, or damages of any kind to person, including death, and property resulting in whole or in part, directly or indirectly, from the acceptance, possession, misuse, or use of the prizes, or participation in this sweepstakes. By entering the sweepstakes, the winner's parent/legal guardian consents to of the use of the winner's name, likeness, and biographical data for publicity and promotional purposes on behalf of Random House, Inc., or FremantleMedia with no additional compensation or further permission (except where prohibited by law). Other entry names will NOT be used for subsequent mail solicitation. For the names of the winners, available after December 15, 2002, please send a stamped, self-addressed envelope to: American Idol "You Be the Judge," Random House Children's Books, 1540 Broadway, 19th Floor, New York, NY 10036. Washington and Vermont residents may omit return postage.

Sponsor of this Sweepstakes is Random House, Inc.